W9-CPW-081

Yee Haw!

A BEAR'S VACATION

Written by
Tracey Herrold

Illustrated by
Alexandra Lee

"Yee haw!" shouted Tex the minute he heard the news.

He and his family were going on a vacation.

Tex couldn't wait! It wasn't that he didn't like his cozy cave in Yellowstone Park. It was just that he had run out of things to lasso. He'd roped every tree, every bush, and every critter in the park. He'd even lassoed a few tourists by mistake! And now he'd have a chance to try out his lasso in the big city!

Tex packed his hat and his boots and he circled
up his very best lasso. "There'll be some mighty
fine wrangling going on in the city," he said,
throwing the lasso over his shoulder.

"There'll be some wrangling all right," Ma
said. "But remember, the city is a big place. It's
not like our cozy cave. You'll need to pay
attention or you'll get lost."

"Yes, Ma," Tex said, closing up his suitcase.
"Yee haw!" he added, just for fun.

Next morning, a bus pulled up in front of their cave. Tex let out one of his famous "Yee haws!" and the Brownbear family piled in.

"Ma?" asked Tex, once they were settled in their seats. "What kind of horses do they have in the city? Will I get to do any of my rope tricks?"

"I'm sure you'll get to try out some of your wrangling, Tex," Ma answered. "But remember to pay attention! I don't want you getting lost!"

During the long bus ride, Tex looked out the window. He saw lots of things he could lasso. There were horses and cows, pigs and tractors. . . . Tex closed his eyes and imagined all the things he might lasso with his long rope.

Soon he had fallen asleep.

When Tex opened his eyes, he was in the big city! There were tall, tall buildings, so tall he could barely see their tops. There were bright, bright lights. And there were people everywhere.

Ma and Pa took Tex by the hand and together they went off to see the city's sights.

The first thing Tex did was look around for something to lasso. In no time he spotted the perfect target! It was in front of a big building with thick pillars—a statue of a man who was riding . . . a horse! Tex took off for some wrangling.

"Yee haw!" yelled Tex. He pulled out his lasso and twirled it up toward the statue. The lasso looped around the statue's neck.

"Young man," a deep voice said. The voice came from a guard who was suddenly standing near Tex. "That statue is a work of art. It is not to be lassoed. I'm sorry, but I have to ask that you leave here at once."

Tex smiled his widest bear smile. "But sir—" he began.

"At once!" the guard commanded.

Tex turned and headed back to his parents—
only his parents weren't there!

"Hmmm," said Tex. "I bet they went to
the zoo."

He circled up his lasso, threw it over his
shoulder, and followed the signs that said "Big
City Zoo."

When he got to the gates of the zoo, Tex couldn't believe his eyes. There, in front of the entrance, was a police officer—and he was on top of a horse!

Tex just couldn't help himself. He grabbed his lasso and swung. The lasso sailed up in the air and landed perfectly around the horse's neck.

"Yee haw!" Tex yelled.

"Now son," the police officer said sternly. "I'm here to protect you and I can't do that if my horse has a rope around its neck."

"I understand, sir," Tex said. "But isn't there some wrangling I can do inside the zoo?"

"You know," the officer replied. "I'm not sure the zoo is really up to a visit from a wild west bear. Where are your parents? And what are you doing wandering around this big city by yourself?"

Tex looked up and down the busy street that ran in front of the zoo.

"I don't rightly know," he said. "I'll go look in the park."

Tex followed the signs that said "Big City
Park." When he got to the park's gates, he heard
a big commotion.

"Stop them!" someone shouted. "Stop them
at once!"

Over the hill came two horses, turning their
heads left and right as they ran. Behind the
horses was a carriage. Behind the carriage ran
a man with a tall top hat and a long whip. The
horses were heading straight for a swing set.

"Watch out!" someone yelled. "The horses are out of control!"

Tex took one look at the horses and knew what he had to do. He grabbed his lasso.

Then he let out one big "Yee haw!" With all of his might, he threw the lasso around one of the horses' necks. Both horses slowed to a canter. Then they slowed to a trot. Then, just as they were about to reach the playground, they stopped altogether.

By that time a crowd had gathered. The man with the tall hat and whip walked up to Tex. "Young man," he said, "you're a hero! You stopped my horses from running into that playground. If they had kept going, they might have injured some children."

Tex just smiled. "My pleasure, pardner," he said. "Just a little wild west hospitality."

"Tex!" called someone from the crowd. It was Ma Brownbear.

She ran up to him. Pa was right behind.

"We were so worried about you!" Ma said. "I told you to pay attention."

"But madame," the carriage driver said. "He *was* paying attention. After all, if he hadn't been, he wouldn't have seen my runaway horses."

"I guess you're right," Pa answered. "You were paying attention, Tex. And your lasso came in mighty handy."

Tex grinned his widest bear grin. Then he yelled out, "Yee haw!"

Tex spent the rest of the afternoon showing off all of his fancy rope tricks. The crowd gasped as he twirled the rope high over his head. They roared when he jumped in and out of the circles he twirled.

And they laughed when he roped a tourist who was walking down the street. By the end of the day, they were all yelling "Yee haw!" just like Tex.

Soon, the bear family had to leave Big City and head back to Yellowstone. Before they hopped on their bus, they said goodbye to their favorite carriage driver. There he was, with a crowd around him, doing the fancy rope tricks he had learned from Tex.

"Yee haw!" he shouted. "Come back anytime!
You're good for business."
"Yee haw!" Tex yelled back.

 And then he climbed on the bus and headed
back to the park with his family for their long
winter's nap.